I0571196

SECRET TO SOMEWHERE

Mystery at the Old Mission

A Justi Wallace/Christopher Williams Adventure

By Eloise E. Kraemer

Haumea Publishing Co.

Mystery at the Old Mission

DEDICATION

This story is dedicated to the young people of the world in hopes that they will continue with perpetual curiosity, searching for, and uncovering unsolved mysteries of the past while respecting laws and rules of the present; all the while, endeavoring to embrace today's technological advances and educational opportunities.

Life is short. Embrace it.

Secret to Somewhere

CONTENTS

Secret to Somewhere

ACKNOWLEDGEMENTS

I wish to thank the Coeur d'Alene Tribal Council and the Old Mission State Park for giving me a better grasp of the history of the area and the importance of following procedures in relation to treasure hunting.

All characters in this story are purely fictional, except the famous Butch Cassidy, reputed to have gone by Robert Le Roy Parker and Le Roy Parker. I derived some of the information about Robert Le Roy Parker, or Butch Cassidy from a book by Dora Flack as told by Lula Parker, "Butch Cassidy, My Brother".

The letter in this book from L. Parker is purely imaginary. Rock Creek and Silver Creek, Idaho are an imaginary blend of several small towns running the length of the Silver Valley of Northern Idaho including Mullan, Wallace, Kellogg, Smelterville, Pinehurst and Kingston.

The Mission of the Sacred Heart or Cataldo Mission or Old Mission, Cataldo, Idaho, now a

State Park, was constructed between 1850 and 1853 and is Idaho's oldest standing building. In 1961 it was designated a National Historic Landmark, and in 1966 it was put on the National Register of Historic Places.

The First National Bank of Winnemucca still stands at 352 Bridge Street, Winnemucca, Nevada. It closed its doors to banking in December of 1932 during the Great Depression.

Inspiration for the Sixth Street Café came from the De Lashmutt Building, in Wallace, Idaho. It was built in 1890 after a fire destroyed the downtown section of the city of Wallace. The building served as the Shoshone County Courthouse from 1898 to 1905. Portions of the building subsequently served as a post office, a millinery, a drugstore, a clothing store and, the most popular, a cigar store. It also served as a bar and a restaurant. The apartments above were rented to boarders. The De Lashmutt Building is on the National Historic Register.

It is said, that buried somewhere along the old Mullan Road between Wallace, Idaho and Spokane Falls, Washington, there lies a treasure of $32,640. This treasure was supposedly stolen from the First National Bank of Winnemucca in September of 1900.

Stories say that Butch Cassidy was part of the gang that robbed the bank.

Maybe he was.

Chapter 1

New Summer Digs

Christopher Williams was not in the best of moods. He pushed a mop around his brother, David's new restaurant, the Sixth Street Cafe.

This was not how Christopher planned on spending his summer. It was the summer he would turn sixteen.

"Oh, this is just great!" Christopher thought.

"I can boast that I held the position of janitor in chief! That should look really great on my resume. What more can I ask for?"

Irritation flickered through his thoughts as

he dunked the mop in water and wrung it out.

Most of his friends were hanging out at the lake this summer, partying and having fun.

His friend, Tyler, had a job at his father's computer repair business. Justi, his lifelong best friend and confidant, probably was helping out at the Sheriff's office, where her dad had her type reports and file when he was behind in his work, or short of help.

When Christopher agreed to help his brother out, he pictured fishing, kayaking on the river, biking on the many trails that had been constructed on the old railroad beds that were no longer used for railroads, and hiking trails into mountain lakes.

He was also an avid reader and had planned on catching up on his reading over the summer.

Of course, he knew that his brother needed some help with the new business. That was part of the agreement when Dave asked Christopher to stay.

Dave, and his wife, Jenny, had just purchased their dream restaurant business in the small town of Silver Creek, Idaho. Jenny was pregnant with their first child.

Christopher was happy to help out and be there when his little nephew was born. Dave and Jenny had even asked Christopher to pick the name of his future nephew, since the baby was due to be born September 12th, which was the same date of Christopher's sixteenth birthday.

Christopher had been given a choice of Mark or Adam for the new baby's name.

Christopher chose Mark. He thought Mark sounded like a strong name. He could picture teaching Mark to fish and hunt someday.

"Of course," Christopher fantasized, "Dave will be there when he can, to teach little Mark, but, I'm sure that Dave will be far too busy in the restaurant to give Mark all the *guidance* he will need as he grows older."

"That will be when I, as the uncle, will step in to attend to the more exciting adventures as he grows!"

Christopher was frustrated with all this restaurant "busy work," though. He hadn't envisioned all these mundane chores!

"Why can't Dave just hire a janitor to take care of the restaurant dishes, table cleanups, mopping, window washing and sign placing?" Christopher grumbled.

He actually knew the answer. Money was always the problem. Things were tight.

On top of everything else, Jennifer was having a difficult pregnancy and had to rest much more than had been anticipated.

"Oh well, it is what it is," thought Christopher.

He pushed the mop under the counters, cleaning spills from the morning's customers. A shock of dark brown hair fell over his brow. He brushed it back in a quick motion, a habit he had when he was anxious or frustrated.

His hair was neatly trimmed over his ears and at his neck, but was thick and soft and had a slightly tousled look to the forefront.

Christopher's eyes were large, soft and brown, yet they could almost glow with an inner light if he was excited, surprised or upset.

He had a strong jaw with ever so slight of a cleft, high cheekbones and an aquiline nose that fit well with his features.

Overall, Christopher was a striking young man, tall for 16, slim and well muscled. He had put on a lot of height this past year. His mother was always complaining that he couldn't "keep his shirts tucked in," or that his pants "had shrunk again."

"Maybe, Justi will call tonight. Maybe, her aunt and uncle will ask her up for the weekend," mused Christopher.

Justi's Aunt Mae and Uncle Walt Wallace owned the local hardware store in Silver Creek. Justi's parents and Christopher's parents had both been born and raised in Silver Creek, a small mining and logging community in the northern part of Idaho.

Justi's grandfather and grandmother, Eric and Peggy Wallace, owned the hardware store in Silver Creek while Justi's father and her Uncle Walter were growing up. When

Eric and Peggy retired, their son and daughter-in-law, Walter and Mae Wallace, had purchased the store.

Christopher couldn't remember life without Justi hanging around. They had started kindergarten together. Their mother's had been friends in college, and the children had play dates together when they were just toddlers.

Justi had also grown and changed quite a bit in the last couple of years.

She had grown from a short, scrawny tomboy into a charming young lady. Justi was still on the thin side, and was still not as tall as many of her classmates, but she still could out-hike many a boy.

What Christopher missed most about Justi was her spirit.

He loved way her large blue eyes, with just the smallest dots of green in them, could light up with a mischievous, "Cheshire Cat" look.

Her smile, which always crinkled her nose just a tad, brightened the dullest of days, and could change the mood in a room in the blink of an eye.

Her laugh sounded like bits of crystal falling amongst small bells ringing.

Her curiosity was insatiable.

Most of all, her long, tawny blond hair with strands of caramel running through it was like a million rays of sunshine when she flipped it over her shoulders, or tossed her head in a careless gesture.

Christopher liked Justi, but was not anxious, yet, to risk the possibility of losing his best friend by making her his girlfriend.

Justi and Christopher's hometown, North River, Idaho, was only about seventy miles away, but it seemed like a million miles to a fifteen, almost sixteen year old.

Christopher put the mop away and dumped the grey water down the drain in the back room.

As he rinsed the last of the water down the drain, he remembered there were dishes waiting in the sink from the last of the lunch customers. His brother had left him to watch the restaurant, while he ran home to check on Jennifer.

The bright spot in Christopher's job was that his brother had designated him as "chief milkshake maker."

Christopher was allowed to make various flavors of milkshake, within reason, requested by customers. He was also allowed to make himself one if he got hungry. The strangest request he had received was a raisin, peanut butter milkshake with a hint of orange.

He could also help himself to snacks whenever his hunger moved him toward the shelves stocked with pies, cakes, and chips or the refrigerator with burgers to fry. The candy bars were stocked by a separate vendor, and those were off limits unless Christopher paid for them.

Christopher also looked forward to his evenings. He was staying with his grandmother and grandfather, Doug and Ellie Williams. They had both been raised in Silver Creek and loved the mountains and wildlife. They were also *book worms*.

They encouraged Christopher to spend as much time as possible in the outdoors, fishing, hiking, biking and canoeing. They took him on evening hikes into the nearby mountains, or biking when their arthritis allowed it.

They also encouraged him to spend time reading, so they didn't get upset when his night reading light was on into the wee hours of the morning, unless he was slow to get up to help his brother at his restaurant in the morning.

Christopher loved his room at his grandparent's home. It was the same room his father had when he was growing up in Silver Creek.

In the closet, there were still mementos of his dad's days growing up. There were old "Tonka" trucks, a jar of marbles, an old leather baseball mitt and wooden bat, and a letter sweater from Silver Creek High, home of the Miners.

The curtains and bedspread sported the early "Star Wars" characters from his father's childhood.

There were not many dishes left from a

mid-week group of businessmen and local storekeepers that routinely stopped by for lunch. More customers stopped by on Fridays and the weekend, when tourists roamed the town.

As he began collecting the dishes to be cleaned, rinsed and placed in the dishwasher, his mind wandered off towards the milkshake maker sitting idle on the counter.

Christopher had just enough change in his pocket for a candy bar.

"Maybe I should purchase a "Mounds" bar, throw in some vanilla bean Ice cream, some of those fresh strawberries, and some caramel sauce................."

"Mmmmmmm....Yep.....that should make life seem a little sweeter."

Christopher took a milkshake glass off the shelf and set about adding the ingredients.

"Hey! WHAT in the..........!"

Christopher jumped and knocked a cup off the rack. It bounced twice on the floor, rolled and hit the edge of the antique brass foot rail that wrapped around the bottom edge of the lunch bar.

"Oh, my goodness!

"I am just soooooo sorry...........but you looked incredibly silly as you jumped a mile when I tickled you on the neck with this old feather duster!"

It was Justi!

Christopher couldn't believe his eyes.

Chapter 2

Here's Mud in Your Eye

"This changes everything!" thought Christopher.

"Having Justi here is the best!"

Even chores could be fun if you had someone to do them with.

Justi interrupted his thoughts as she placed the feather duster back on the shelf by the cash register.

"As long as you're making milkshakes, you might as well whip me up one."

"It would be really nice if you could make it chocolate, peanut butter and jelly!"

"Okay," responded Christopher, "As long as you finish up the dishes in the sink!"

"I put the gloves by the coffee maker. Be sure to rinse them well, and then they go into the

17

dishwasher. Glasses go on the top rack."

"So, do you want to know how I happen to be here?" questioned Justi, as she began methodically scraping and rinsing dishes, placing them in the dishwasher.

"Of course, and how long are you staying?" replied Christopher, as he measured ingredients into the milkshake maker.

"Well, I guess, all summer, if they'll have me," was Justi's reply.

Justi went on to explain that her mother had been talking to her sister-in-law, Justi's Auntie Mae. Her mother mentioned that Christopher was spending the summer helping out at the restaurant.

Her mother also happened to mention that Justi was not so happy about the prospect of spending the whole summer without the company of her closest friend.

Auntie Mae and Uncle Walter had soft hearts, and were always the first ones to offer assistance if there was a family problem. Mae also saw this as the answer to the fact that they were a little short of help this summer at the hardware store. Mae and Walter's four year old daughter, Zoey, was quite a handful, and loved to follow her older cousin, Justi around.

Mae had been trying to figure out how to get away from the house with Walter for a movie date once in a while, as well as how to secure more help at the hardware store.

It seemed like Justi was just the answer!

Justi's parents were quick to agree that a summer in Silver Creek helping her aunt and uncle might be just the cure for Justi's blues.

They made Mae and Walter agree to place some reasonable restrictions on Justi's adventure time with her best friend Christopher, and promise to make her responsible by giving her a decent amount of chores around the house and at the store.

Justi was ecstatic about the arrangement.

By the time she had explained how she came to be in Silver Creek to Christopher, both milkshakes had disappeared and Christopher was cleaning up the glasses.

Christopher's brother came in just as he picked up the broom to sweep the floor.

"Justi, I just heard from the local grapevine that you're here for the summer. Sweet!"

"Why don't you two get out of here early tonight, so you have a chance to catch up on the happenings back home in North River?"

Christopher and Justi didn't argue. After removing his apron, Christopher joined Justi outside the restaurant. Both had ridden their bikes from home.

They rode together to Justi's aunt and uncle's house. Aunt Mae was in the front yard with little Zoey when they rode up.

"Just the girl I was looking for," laughed Aunt Mae.

"I was wondering if you could watch little Zoey after dinner tonight so Walt and I can go out to the movies tonight. It has been ages since we have had a date together. "

"That's fine, Aunt Mae," agreed Justi.

"Can we take Zoey to the park to play before dinner?"

"Certainly," replied Aunt Mae.

"Just be sure to be back by five o'clock, and try not to let Zoey get too dirty, I bathed her after her nap and she has her little outfit on I got her for her birthday last month. I thought I could get you to snap some pictures of her with her dad and me when Walt gets home. We don't have any recent ones of the three of us, and I wanted to send some out to family."

Justi and Christopher assured Aunt Mae they would take extra care of Zoey so her outfit would stay reasonably clean.

That was the plan.

When they got to the park, Zoey went over to the sand pile and proceeded to dig with a little sand shovel. She was singing to herself, having the greatest time finding sticks for "little people" and dandelions to place around a small hole she had decided was to be her garden.

Justi and Christopher sat on the swings and talked about friends and what they were all doing this summer.

It was a beautiful summer afternoon. The sun was warm, and the world seemed to be in perfect order. The two friends were together again, talking about what they might do with the rest of the summer.

The voice of Zoey was a sweet hum in the background as she talked to the sticks like they were real people.

All of a sudden, Justi realized that she no longer heard Zoey talking to her sticks. She glanced at where she had seen Zoey moments before, busily tucking dandelions into the sand for her garden plants. Zoey was nowhere to be seen!

Jumping out of the swing, with Christopher close behind, she screamed Zoey's name, "Zoey, ZOEY! Where did you go?"

"I oder heeeeere………" came the faint sound of Zoey from behind some nearby bushes.

"I falled in the mud and got kinda messy. I think

I kinda got stuck!"

"Oh no, Zoey!"

There stood Zoey.

Zoey looked more like a moving piece of mud than a child named Zoey.

Zoey had wandered over to a little puddle made by a sprinkler that was broken. She had a paper cup she had found in the sand pile. She decided to get some water for her pretend "flower garden".

There was a spider in the bottom of the cup. Zoey busied herself picking the spider out of the cup as she walked toward the puddle of water, singing pieces of the little song, "Itsy Bitsy Spider".

The puddle was mostly soft, slippery mud.

The edges of the puddle were soft with squishy clay-like mud.

Zoey had to wade out to the middle of the puddle to get enough water to scoop up. The water partially covered her shoes when she stopped to survey the situation.

Zoey knew she should keep clean. Mama and cousin Justi would not be happy if she got any mud on her nice shoes or dress.

She already had some mud on the bottoms and sides of her shoes, but she figured that she could wipe that off on the grass. Zoey sized up the situation as thoughtfully as a small child can.

She thought she could probably just barely get enough water if she reached very hard as far as she could toward the middle of the pond while she stood very still, not going further into the muddy puddle.

She was just stretching her chubby little hand as far as her arm could stretch to scoop up the murky water when a dog ran by barking ferociously at a squirrel.

Zoey, surprised by the commotion, dropped her cup and fell face first into the muddy water!

Her pretty little pink birthday outfit was now dripping with brownish orange clay colored mud.

Her bright golden curls were slimy brownish

orange. Here cute little white shoes and socks were soaked and covered in the same dark muddy slime.

Justi and Christopher looked at each other in horror. Christopher walked over and carefully picked up woeful little Zoey.

"Don't you worry, Zoey! Your cousin, Justi, will have you cleaned up in no time!"

The shadow of a devilish grin flickered over his face.

Justi had her first lesson in responsibility.

There would be no pictures for the Wallace family tonight.

Justi tried to make it up to her aunt and uncle by volunteering to not only clean up Sara before dinner, but to clean up the dinner dishes, clean Zoey's muddied clothes, and to babysit that evening.

She tucked in Zoey that night, with a nice bedtime story about a little bear that got himself into much the same sort of trouble. The bear's story had a happy ending.

Zoey was so tired by the experience that she was asleep in no time.

Aunt Mae and Uncle Walter enjoyed their date. Justi was asleep on the couch when they got home, dreaming of the summer days to come, adventuring with Christopher.

Chapter 3

Out of the Alley

Christopher left Justi and Zoey at the Wallace's, and rode his bike home to his grandparent's house.

Christopher's grandmother had already left to play pinochle with some other ladies at the senior center.

He watched television with his grandfather and he and his grandfather ate frozen meals.

His grandfather didn't have much to say when he watched television. He had his favorite old shows like "Magnum P.I." or "N.C.I.S." or just news programs. Grandpa watched a lot of news.

Christopher gave up on his grandfather after the third news program came on.

"I think I'll head up to bed, Grandpa."

"Okay, son…goodnight," responded Grandpa as he took another sip of his, now cold, coffee.

Christopher wondered, "How can he still drink that cold coffee? It sits in the pot all day long. He heats it up in the microwave, then he lets it sit on the side table and get cold, then he slowly drinks it…….Yuuuck!"

Christopher climbed the stairs to his bedroom, thinking about the coming weekend. He hoped to be able to spend it with Justi.

Maybe they could go hiking up to Mt. Baldy.

As he entered the room, the orange glow from his father's old "Star Wars" lamp welcomed him.

 The familiar scent in the room, reminded him of all the years he had stayed in this very room, even in a crib as an infant, when his family visited Grams and Gramps.

The scent was warm and comforting, like wrapping up in an old blanket.

He opened the closet door. His father's old trunk stood with the lid still open. Christopher sat down beside it and looked through several old novels, inside, searching for something good to read.

There were a couple of old school albums belonging to his father, from Silver Creek High, home of the "Miners". He paged through them, thoughtfully, looking for pictures of his father and mother.

"Gee, they sure looked different, back then!"

He wondered what he and Justi would look like twenty-some years from now.

"I'll probably be bald, and she will probably still have that same smile!"

He picked out an old novel, shut off the light in the closet and closed the door.

The lamp cast an eerie glow on the walls of the bedroom where some ancient posters still hung.

Two of the posters were of old movies from his parents' time; "Beetlejuice" and "The Breakfast Club".

"Huh," thought Christopher, "Maybe Justi and I should stop by the library one of these evenings and see if they have a copy of those old movies. It would be interesting to see what people our parent's age thought was "cool" back then.

He got ready for bed and opened up the book he had chosen out of his father's collection.

The book was a science fiction about a boy that had stowed away on a pirate's space ship.

Christopher started finding it hard to keep his eyes open just as the book took a suspenseful turn.

The space pirates were just about to discover the stowaway.

He lost the battle with sleep as his eyes closed one last time, his mind drifting off into the mists.

He became the stowaway on a spaceship that looked suspiciously like one out of an old "Star Wars" movie, as the pirates discovered him mopping the floor with a blue milkshake in one hand.

Their swords were drawn as they advanced. A warning alarm sounded aboard the ship. The alarm sounded more and more like birds chirping.

When Christopher awoke on Saturday morning, it was to the sound of birds scolding a cat outside of his window.

He smelled pancakes and bacon wafting up from the kitchen, and heard the sound of his Grandpa's footsteps on the porch as he left to get the paper at the gate.

"Good morning, sleepyhead!" chimed Grandma, as he entered the kitchen.

"It's already 8:10 and your brother said to make sure you were down at the restaurant by 9:30. He promised Jennifer he would go crib shopping today in Coeur d'Alene. He wants you to mind the restaurant after the noon rush until three p.m. today."

Christopher groaned. He was hoping to go exploring with Justi today after lunch. Oh well, it would just have to wait until he got off work.

"If Justi calls, would you please tell her to meet me at the Sixth Street Cafe, Grandma?"

"Certainly, I will, dear. It is so nice you two are

both able to have some time together this summer."

"Yeah," responded Christopher, "I just hope our jobs don't get in the way of some good adventures!"

Grandma laughed, "Somehow, I'm sure you will be able to work in plenty of trouble!"

Christopher kicked a round rock down the alley like a small soccer ball as he made his way to his brother's restaurant. It rolled like a wobbly tire, hitting a garbage can at the back of a neighboring store.

A plaintive "meow" sounded from behind a cardboard box that sat against the can.

Christopher walked toward the box and nudged it with his foot. A very tiny black kitten with white paws and a white chin poked its head out of the box.

"Well, hello there, little feller'! What are you doing down there?" exclaimed Christopher, as he bent down and picked up the miniature fur ball.

A loud purring erupted from the tiny creature. It

softly nuzzled its small, damp nose into the palm of his hand and rubbed its head on his thumb.

Christopher's heart went to mush.

"Okay, little fellow, let's see if you might want a bowl of milk!"

Christopher tucked the kitten into the front of his hooded sweat shirt as he stepped into the back door of the restaurant.

His brother was busy with a customer, so Christopher stepped behind the bar and poured a small bowl of milk. He grabbed a towel from the bar and quietly carried the milk bowl, kitten and towel to the back room and down into the basement.

The basement was a large room that resembled a cave more than a room. It was also a room without end, since, after the walls were dug out and shored up with bricks and stone, in the early 1900s, they continued to dig under the streets to adjoin other businesses. The walls were not finished. The building basically sat on pilings and stone cornerstones. The furnace sat to one side about three feet away from the stairwell.

To the left of the stairwell, there was one room with a door that had been more or less finished out as a storeroom in later years.

Christopher opened this door and placed the kitten and the dish of milk on the floor in the corner. He took an empty cardboard box from the shelf and placed the kitchen towel in it for the kitten. He placed the kitten in the box with a loving pat.

"There you go, little guy! Now, be quiet and take a nice nap while I help Dave. We'll deal with your future tonight."

Christopher quietly shut the store room door and headed back up the basement stairs to help his brother.

After the noon rush of customers, David and Jennifer left for Coeur d'Alene for an afternoon of shopping. Christopher busied himself with sweeping, re-setting tables and doing dishes.

When Justi arrived at three, Christopher took her to the basement to see the kitten after locking up the restaurant.

"I think you should name him Alley," suggested Justi, "because he came from the alley!"

"Yes, that's a great name. Look, he's purring and rubbing your leg! I think he likes his name."

Just then, the kitten darted past Justi's legs and out into the main part of the basement.

Several boxes were stacked against the old rock and concrete walls. The far part of the basement opened out into the area most resembling a cave with posts shoring up the floors and dirt for walls in areas leading to a tunnel and a door. There was a multitude of corners and crannies for a small kitten to hide.

Just then, paper rustled behind a cardboard box sitting next to a large trunk against a brick wall.

Justi jumped as the kitten softly mewed from behind the boxes.

Chapter 4

Where Spiders Creep and Cobwebs Sleep

Christopher and Justi closed in on the pile of old boxes. Just as Justi started to pick up the box where the mewing had come from, the kitten scurried behind the old trunk.

Christopher made a football type dive-tackle, for the end of the trunk to shut off the kitten's escape to the far end of the room. He smashed into the side of the trunk, hitting his head and shoulder against the brick wall.

"Ouch! That was not planned!" shouted Christopher as the trunk skidded sideways, leaving an opening for the kitten to escape.

Justi grabbed the kitten just as it made its rush for freedom.

"Gottcha, little feller!" exclaimed Justi, as she

tucked the kitten in her arms and calmed him with soft strokes.

She put Alley back into the storeroom, shutting the door tightly.

Christopher began picking up the old magazines that had been stacked on top of the trunk.

"Look, these are old "National Geographic" magazines from the 1960s. They are still in really good shape. We should see if your brother wants to donate them to the local library," suggested Justi.

"That's a good idea," responded Christopher, as he placed them in a stack beside the trunk.

He pulled the trunk out into the room and opened the lid. It stood, annoyingly empty, with a strong scent of dampness and mold.

Disappointed in the empty trunk, Christopher closed the lid and began to push it back against the wall, when he discovered that his fall had dislodged a couple of bricks and some mortar in the old wall.

A couple of bricks wobbled loosely and another

brick and loose mortar chunked down on top of the trunk as he pushed it against the wall, leaving a sizeable hole in the structure.

The hole revealed a small room about the size of a walk in closet.

Armed with a flashlight retrieved from the storage room, Christopher and Justi pulled loose a couple more bricks and crawled through the hole in the wall to explore.

Under shelves to the back of the room was another old trunk. As Justi opened it, she was aware of the same distinct old musty stench held by the other trunk.

It was apparent the trunk had not been opened for a very long time. Under an old quilt, was a neatly folded and stacked arrangement of clothing, including ancient corsets and long white gloves, adorned with small white pearl buttons.

Neat cotton dresses were long and embellished with many ruffles, tiny buttons, lacing and ribbing.

All of the dresses appeared extremely petite.

"I think these clothes are from back as far as maybe even in the early 1900s!" exclaimed Justi.

"Back then, ladies were smaller built because they weren't fed as well as we are now."

"They look like some clothing I saw in the museum in North River!"

As Justi picked up the last dress, a yellowed envelope fell out and to the floor. A miniature brass key, the shape of a skeleton key, fell out of the envelope and into the dust on the floor.

Christopher picked up the small brass colored key and turned it over in his hand. The key had a red string on it.

"This looks like an old luggage key of some sort," he speculated.

Justi removed a faded old letter from the envelope and unfolded it. The writing was apparently done with quill and ink and had lightened over the years.

Justi and Christopher squinted in the narrow beam of the flashlight as they read the following letter together

This day, October 23, 1900

Dearest Dolly,

Sorry, we weren't able to stop to visit on our way through.

I met up with Etta in Missoula. We took the train to Dudley. We might have continued on to Spokane, but Etta had it in her mind to visit friends in Coeur d'Alene. This means we needed to take the steamboat downstream.

At Dudley Station, there were lots of Pinkertons mulling 'round. I suppose it's from the unrest in the area from mining strikes and riots. I guess they had a big blow-up last year that got everyone's attention. No one is very trusting it won't happen again

We received word the steamboat had some trouble in Harrison and would not arrive until late this evening, so we took the ferry to the Mission of the Sacred Heart where we were assured we could enjoy the hospitality of the priests while we waited.

In any case, this side trip allowed us to remove ourselves from the survey of Pinkertons, and gave us some time to think of options, being rather nervous of the goods we carry in Etta's new leather hatbox. The hatbox would have been quite a burden for Etta to tote it around in any such ladylike fashion, so I carried it for her, tucked under my arm, so as not to divulge the excess weight.

We walked up the hill to the Mission and

beheld a beautiful setting.

Etta and I sat a while out front, listening to some singing. There was a squeezebox player playin' pretty sweet tunes. We had a box dinner to enjoy as did many of the others from the train waiting for the steamboat. The priests offered coffee and the sweetest tasting water fresh from the mountains.

I got to thinking I needed to find a nice place for the leather hatbox before we took the riverboat to the town of Coeur d'Alene.

I stepped off the left side of the Mission's front porch with the hatbox tucked underneath my arm, and kinda' mosied across the pasture to the west of the mission toward old fencepost made from probably a railroad tie. An old crow was sittin' on top of it making quite a

racket. What do you know, an old pick was
sitting by the post. I kinda' used it to prop
me up heading down the hill and through the
mission graveyard. I rested a minute beside a
headstone in the graveyard, considering my
options. I sighted a small grove of fir saplings
the priests had planted down the hill a bit, at
the west end of the graveyard.

As I walked down to the saplings, I noticed
that bushes at the edge of the graveyard hid me
well from prying eyes. One sapling appeared
to be joining his close friend in growth,
making two trees one. I stepped out five paces
in a northwesterly direction of this odd little
tree and proceeded to dig me a hole. I dug
about quite a time till I had scratched about
two feet into the sandy soil. I had my rain
slicker on since the mornings and evenings

have a bit of a chill. I just kinda' wrapped the leather hatbox really good in that old slicker and stuffed it into the hole. The river winds its way around, and just below it appears to make a bit of an eddy near the bank. There was a huge beaver house by the bank that seemed about in line with that there little tree. My pocket watch reads a little slow, but, I'm figuring it was approximately 4:30 in the evening. The setting sun lined up with that little tree, and that really huge beaver house.

Now, if I don't seem to reappear after this Alaska trip, and you don't get another letter, I want you to try to recover the loot. Please keep some for yerself for all the trouble and please give the rest to the nice priests for the Schit su'umsh, or Coeur d'Alene Indians at the Mission and maybe some for someone that takes in kids with no place to go, or helps them learn things. I always liked kids.

Keep safe,

Your friend, L. Parker

A Plaintive meowing came from the storeroom.

"I think Alley is saying he deserves credit for this find," laughed Justi.

Chapter 5

A Home for Alley

Justi suggested she take Alley to Aunt Mae and Uncle Walter's home to see if it could become a companion for her niece, Zoey.

Christopher agreed that this sounded like a good idea, since the kitten couldn't stay in the storeroom at the restaurant forever.

Justi scooped up Alley and headed up the basement stairs with Christopher.

As they walked home together, they discussed their discovery behind the brick wall. The kitten cuddled contentedly in Justi's arms, purring softly.

"Who do you think this man, L. Parker was? Do you think we will ever be able to find out? Maybe he was some famous robber or something," speculated Justi.

"Maybe he was a burglar and no one ever knew who he was," retorted Christopher.

"Or a stage robber or a train robber," fantasized Justi.

"Well, maybe we should start by looking to see if anything was buried around here from any old robberies, or if anything was dug up around an old mission. I think I remember hearing that there is a mission around here somewhere." Christopher mused.

After agreeing to meet at the local library on Monday evening, Christopher and Justi said their goodbyes at Justi's aunt and uncle's gate.

Zoey was overjoyed when she saw the kitten. Justi's aunt and uncle agreed to keep Alley on a trial basis, when they saw how much fun Zoey was having with the kitten.

Justi rigged up a piece of yarn with a feather on it for Zoey to pull along. The kitten pounced after it while Zoey giggled uncontrollably.

Chapter 6

Counting Cows Instead of Sheep

The phone rang Sunday morning just as Justi, her aunt and uncle and Zoey were headed out to church. It was Christopher.

"Hey, Justi, I just found out that we are going up to my Uncle Rob's ranch this afternoon. Grandma and Grandpa say you can go with us if you want to. We can ride horses and go fishing."

"That's great!" exclaimed Justi, "You are on speaker phone, since we are heading to church and Auntie and Uncle are both nodding their heads in unison."

Aunt Mae chimed in, "We can drop her off after church, just be sure she is back by no later than 9:00 p.m. this evening. Justi has to help us in the hardware store tomorrow."

That afternoon Justi and Christopher rode out on the horses with Christopher's grandfather. Grandpa had promised Christopher's Uncle Rob that he would help him find some missing cows. Uncle Rob and Aunt Jill had a ranch south of Cataldo, Idaho.

The ranch was on about eighty acres and included long sloping meadows with many small draws folded into the landscape. The land gently climbed into the south slope of Baldy Mountain which was timbered in several species of pine and fir. There was also some cedar and black cottonwood down by the river. It was also loaded with bushes and rocks where stealthy mother cows loved to hide away with the elk and deer to have their young.

A large creek tumbled its way from the mountainside down through the meadow and to the river below.

Grandpa, Justi and Christopher were covering the south mountainside and upper creek, while Uncle Rob and Aunt Jill were going to take the meadow and creek bottom.

"Grandpa, have you ever heard any stories about gold being buried around here or any historical bank or train robberies?" Christopher queried.

"Sure, there are lots of stories. An old military trail ran through this valley at one time. The Union Pacific had a rail line with a depot close to Cataldo back in the late 1800s. Steamboats used to come up the river from Coeur d'Alene and surrounding towns to the south like Harrison and Plummer." There was a good amount of gold and ore being shipped in the valley and the banks had lots of money in them, but I'm not sure about any specific bank or train robberies.

"I do think I remember hearing of some gold buried somewhere between here and Spokane Washington by Butch Cassidy, but who knows about stories like that."

Christopher and Justi exchanged knowing looks. They said nothing.

Just about then, they heard some rustling in the bushes and a long low "mooo". Standing over a small wet lump on the ground was a large black mother cow with a spot of white about the size of a tennis ball on her forehead. On her side was white slash that appeared like a question mark at first glance. There was a RJ) brand on the right rump.

"That's old Riddler!" exclaimed Grandpa.

"She was born with that white question mark on her side. It looked real clear when she was first born. She was bottle fed. Aunt Jill named her the Riddler. She used to follow everyone around when she was a young calf."

The wet lump unfolded and stood up on wobbly legs. It started searching for some milk from mother cow. The Riddler's long wet tongue started licking the calf's wet head, ears, neck, continuing to encourage the baby as it found milk.

"It looks like Riddler just went off to have a little quiet time and have her little one," whispered Grandpa.

It was the first time Justi had seen a newly born calf. They spent some time taking pictures and watching the calf learn how to nurse, then headed out for where they planned to meet Uncle Rob and Aunt Jill by the creek.

As they came around the last turn on the trail to the creek, a second cow, brown and white, this time, jumped out on the trail, followed by twin calves. They were a little steadier on their feet, but also seemed quite young. The cows headed down the trail in front of the horses, also headed for the creek.

Everyone arrived about the same time to the picnic spot under a large ponderosa pine. Grandma was there with the pickup truck, already setting up lunch. Uncle Rob and Aunt Jill were riding up the creek bottom laughing at the sight of the three cows running ahead of Christopher, Justi and Grandpa.

"I see you've invited your friends for lunch!" hollered Grandma, as they rode up.

After lunch, Justi and Christopher went down to the creek to look for frogs.

"I wish I had brought my fish pole," pouted Justi.

"Oh yeah, and where would you have put it on your horse?" laughed Christopher, as he untied his shoelace and pulled it out of his shoe.

Christopher slowly reached into his pocket and pulled out a safety pin. He attached the pin to the end of the shoelace. He fashioned the pin to resemble a fishing hook as best he could. Next, he turned over some rocks, revealing a very large worm.

With his pocket knife, he cut a willow branch and tied the end of the shoelace onto it opposite the end with the with safety pin hook attached. The worm was soon wiggling on the end of the bent pin.

"Do you think you can actually catch a fish with that contraption?"

"I sure do," bragged Christopher, as he tossed the hook out into the stream.

"Well, it seems we have a lead on our research for tomorrow," Justi offered.

"Yep, it does," Christopher agreed, "And this summer has just got a lot more interesting."

A fair sized fish was pulling on his shoelace. Amazing! He still had the touch!

Justi shook her head in disbelief.

Chapter 7

The Place for Questions and Answers

Monday afternoon found Sean Kellogg, assistant librarian at Silver Creek Public Library, busy cataloging some new X-box games that had come in.

"This is great," thought Sean.

"Finally we will have a decent supply of games, both for X-Box and on DVD for the 'pc' so the kids don't have to order and wait for them."

He was glad he had talked the head librarian into keeping more games readily available. The other librarians were not so much into the games, or able to assist patrons that were gaming enthusiasts. Sean was the exception.

Sean's commanding presence contradicted his

quiet personality. He was rather tall, being just less than six foot four. The substantial shadow he cast as he walked among the researchers and gamers in the technology section seemed rather intimidating until newcomers became acquainted with him.

His eyes showed the warmth his words assured. His generous hands danced like a ballerina on the keyboard as he helped gamer enthusiasts with new game recommendations, cheats, hints and codes, and researchers with search ideas and new browsing tools.

The library was Sean's passion. He loved the books, especially the fantasy and science fiction section.

He loved the well arranged technology section, with quiet areas for those doing online research, and pod areas for teenagers into gaming.

He loved the fact that their library provided a small meeting room where students could take online tests or members of the community could meet for small informal meetings with access to a computer.

He loved the technology in the young children's area that was separate from teens and adults and blended with a play area with books and games where children could be easily viewed, or joined by parents.

Sean also loved the unspoken quiet and respect the atmosphere of the library commanded. He loved the people that came into the library with their unending questions and friendly faces. What Sean loved most of all, was helping the patrons.

The patrons loved Sean in return, especially the youngsters, who saw him as a big brother of sorts, who would listen to them and always had a joke or silly story to tell and always had an answer to their technology woes.

Justi was waiting on the bench outside the library when Christopher rode up on his bicycle.

"Hey, Christopher, did you remember that miniature skeleton key?"

"I was thinking that we might be able to look up keys like that and what they were used for back then."

Christopher got a blank look on his face.

"Uh….actually…..I forgot, but…."

His hands went to his jeans pockets, searching first the left, then the right front pocket.

His face lit up with that old Christopher "I'm soooooo good….. Look here!"

His hand shot out of his right jean's pocket with a key dangling between thumb and forefinger.

"Wha laaa! I put the same jeans on that I wore Friday! My Grandma has been after me for not putting things in the wash. She'd kill me if she knew I get as many wears out of them as I can before they get washed!"

"Ehwwwweee!" was all Justi could think of to say.

As they entered the library, they were immediately struck by the contrast between the stately matriarch of a library in their hometown of North River with the creaky oak floors, voluminous bookshelves and ancient lighting that always added to the allure of the answers and secrets held within its walls.

The library did have its modern updates and technology worked into the décor as space permitted making it accessible, welcoming and intriguing.

Not to be forgotten, the irreplaceable personality of Librarian, Mrs. Neely and her aids was the icing on the cake.

In contrast, the Silver Creek Library, being constructed in more recent times, including a later remodel, boasted a modern appeal, with large windows, plants, lower, well spaced bookshelves and ample lighting.

Justi and Christopher were most impressed with the technology area, complete with a research section, separate from the gaming area.

Today the library was extremely quiet with only one library technician on duty.

A rather burley young man with dark rimmed glasses, sandy brown hair, slightly askew and a large grin on his face appeared at the front desk.

He had a black and red gamer T-shirt on with camel pants. He was holding a pair of headphones and splitter.

"Hi there, can I help you folks?"

"Maybe", responded Justi.

"We are doing some research on the area. We are mostly interested in a place called the Mission of the Sacred Heart. I believe there is an old mission somewhere close to here, and we wondered if that is the same one. We'd also like to see if we could find some stories about old bank robberies or railroad robberies or buried treasure around that area."

"Well, that's quite a range," responded Sean.

"By the way, my name is Sean."

"I can point you the way to reference books on the area. As far as the mission, there is the Cataldo Mission not far from here. They also refer to it as the Mission of the Sacred Heart. I believe that was its original name. You can also go on the internet and get a lot of information on that."

"You might even get on the internet and look up about any buried treasure or robberies. Do you have a date or specific town?"

"Well, sort of," responded Justi, looking at Christopher for confirmation on how much information she should be giving Sean.

"My name is Justi Wallace, and this is Christopher Williams, and....uhhh..."

Christopher seemed to be assessing Sean as they talked. He also seemed to come to some sort of conclusion as to Sean's character. He nodded to Justi.

Justi continued, pulling out the old letter, "We found this old letter in the basement of Christopher's brother's restaurant in an old trunk. It looks like it is authentic."

Justi handed Sean the letter.

Sean set down the headphones and adjusted his glasses. "Let's go into this meeting room over here and have a look at this."

After reading over the letter, punctuated by several pauses and exclamations of "Oh, wow!" and "How interesting!" and "Hmmmmm," Sean gave the letter back to Justi and stood up abruptly with an "Okay, let's get busy! You can use this meeting room and the personal computer over there. I'll help you select some books to get started with. This could be a lot of fun. I hope you don't mind if I get involved with this!"

"No, we don't mind at all!" Justi and Christopher responded in unison.

Christopher reached in his pocket and pulled out the miniature skeleton key.

"We found this in the envelope too. We thought we might find out what it is to by looking at similar images on the internet."

"Good idea," responded Sean.

"Christopher, why don't you see if you can find anything on the internet? Justi can help me gather reference books from the Northwest section. Do you either of you have a library card for computer access?"

"Well, we both have cards from North River Library. Will that work?" responded Justi.

Sean assured them that, yes, in fact, both libraries worked together and recognized members from most libraries in the area.

"That's good, because you can check out any materials you need for further research and you can access our computers without a guest pass."

As Christopher poured through internet files, he also learned that Dave's restaurant was built in 1890 and had rooms for rent upstairs for single females. The main floor had been a bar, and a cigar store. At one time it had even been the court house. Tunnels under the building ran under the street and between local businesses. There were also reports of hidden rooms constructed during prohibition in the 1920s through the early 1930s.

It appeared that the trunk had been stowed sometime after "Dolly" had left or passed away, and that she had apparently lived in one of the rooms let to female borders on the second floor of the building.

He poured through images of old luggage keys and found that there were many types of small cases during that period in time that a key such as that might have been made for.

There were old satchels and cases for men and hatboxes and even cases for brushes, combs and mirrors for women.

"Imagine," Christopher thought, "locking away bushes and hats!"

"Justi, Sean!" came the loud whisper of Christopher as he appeared around the edge of the Northwest section of bookshelves.

"I just found out who L. Parker is!"

"I looked up Butch Cassidy and found out that Etta was his girlfriend, Etta Place, and that Butch Cassidy's real name was Robert Leroy Parker!"

"I'll grab the book on Butch Cassidy and the Sundance Kid," responded Sean, his face taking on an incandescent glow.

Returning with the book, it was apparent that Sean had lost some of his enthusiasm.

"I hate to break this to you, but the library closes at five p.m. tonight. The computers will shut down at ten till. It is four-forty-five right now, so we will have to wrap this up tonight."

"Okay, we'll be back tomorrow night, responded Justi."

"Not so fast," replied Christopher, "My parents are coming by tomorrow night."

"Well, I have to babysit on Wednesday night," chimed in Justi.

"I'm off until Friday night," added Sean.

"How about, I save you this room for three o'clock, Friday night. The library stays open until seven on Friday nights. That should give us plenty of time to get something done. I can check out these books on the Cataldo Mission, Butch Cassidy and these two area historical books for you to read up on in the meantime."

"Sounds like a plan," Christopher concluded.

"Too bad I left my 'iPod' at home, but Dave doesn't have internet access set up at the restaurant yet, and the access is so limited at Grams and Gramps, it didn't seem worth it."

Justi added, "Yes, Mom and Dad decided I could go without, as they call it, "playing on the internet," this summer, so they told Auntie and

Uncle to discourage any use at their house. They didn't say I couldn't do research at the library, though!"

.

Chapter 8

Fourth of July with a Bang!

The rest of the week was full of unplanned events.

Christopher's parents decided to extend their stay through the following Wednesday night.

They planned a long camping trip, if you can call staying in a fifth wheel, camping! The fifth wheel was great for pregnant Jennifer, though. She was getting larger by the day and spent more time resting and less time at the restaurant.

Christopher always loved a good camping and fishing trip, but wasn't happy about having to put the mystery on hold.

Justi had to babysit Friday night.

Saturday was quickly filled up for her when her

aunt suggested that they take a camping trip with their boat to Lake Pend 'Oreille.

They had arranged for someone to cover for them at the hardware store, so they wouldn't have to be back until after the Fourth of July.

That's when Justi realized that it was Saturday, JULY 1!

Sean was glad to reschedule the meeting room for the following Friday.

He had caught a summer cold that sent him to bed with some good books for a few days. He said it wasn't too bad, because his window at home looked out towards the area the fireworks would be displayed on the fourth. Besides, he had some "really explosive" computer games he could try out.

It seemed the mystery of the buried treasure was doomed to bide it's time.

Fourth of July found Justi enjoying the water with her little cousin, Zoey, and watching fireworks over Lake Pend 'Oreille, all the while thinking about buried treasure.

Zoey had pleaded until Aunt Mae had relented and brought the kitten, Alley, along.

Justi created a small harness and leash for him.

He didn't seem to mind the leash and busied himself in the sand, pawing around and chasing pinecones.

As soon as the last light had died from the darkened sky from the exploding fireworks over the lake, Justi turned to Aunt Mae.

"May I go into the camper to read, please?"

Uncle Walt handed Justi a roasting stick. "Don't you want to roast some marshmallows for s'mores with Sara first?"

"Oh, well, I guess, okay, maybe just one."

Justi loved s'mores just about more than anything.

She had just melted her first s'more and was ready to take a big bite when she heard a squeal out of Zoey.

Zoey had just been given her s'more and was

walking over to her little chair. Alley was busy chasing a moth, straining at the end of his leash.

All of a sudden, Alley was nowhere to be seen.

Zoey was trying to crawl under the camper, where she had seen Alley scamper.

Uncle Walt fell over his chair in his haste to grab Alley and, or Zoey.

Aunt Mae dropped her marshmallow and stick in the fire. In her confusion, she knocked over her chair, which knocked the table sitting next to it. The table started to wobble, one leg being knocked sideways. Justi grabbed for the package of firecrackers sitting on the edge of the table.

Justi missed. The firecrackers began exploding; crack, crack, snap, bang, BANG! **BANG! BOOM!**

Alley streaked out from under the camper and into some bushes.

Zoey began wailing under the camper.

Uncle Walt pulled himself to his feet, brushing off sand and looking a little dazed.

Aunt Mae screamed and ran for Zoey.

Justi ran towards the bushes, intent on retrieving poor Alley.

Alley was nowhere to be seen. Calling did no good. Food was no match for Alley's fear. Alley wanted nothing to do with camping and campfires that evening.

After the mess was cleaned up and the only sounds that could be heard were the lapping of the lake waters, the crickets and the frogs, Justi thought she could faintly hear some soft little mews, but Alley was not about to give away his hiding spot.

Justi never did get her book, "Butch Cassidy, My Brother" read that night. "Maybe tomorrow," she thought, as she drifted off to sleep.

Meanwhile, Christopher had gone fly fishing with his father, grandfather and brother on the St. Joe River.

While they were out fishing, they ran into an old timer. Christopher asked the elderly gentleman if he knew any stories from the late 1800s about the

Cataldo area.

The old timer told him of the Union Pacific line that ran from Missoula, over the mountain and down through the Valley, to a town called Dudley. Dudley was situated across the river, south of the Cataldo Mission.

He told him of a ferry that crossed to the Mission, and of a steamboat landing near the mission called Mission Landing.

He filled Christopher's imagination with mining wars and soldiers and railroad line detectives called Pinkertons.

Christopher went to sleep that night with more information, more names and more questions and lots of stories to dream about.

Chapter 9

Would You Rather Smell A Skunk or Face A Bear?

A plaintive meowing came from outside the camper the next morning. There was a damp mist in the air. A light fog hung over the lake. Birds were just beginning their morning chirping.

When Justi stepped outside of the camper, a strong scent hit her nose. It took her only moments to recognize the scent.

"I smell a skunk! Awwwwwe yuck!" Justi put her hand up to cover her nose.

Uncle Walt was already out of the camper surveying Alley with disdain as the kitten lapped a bowl of milk and crunched on kitty kibble contentedly.

"Alley is not very discriminating when it comes

to friends," observed Uncle Walt.

"I guess he wanted to do his own celebrating, but he chose a skunk for his friend. Sometime during the night, they must have come to a parting of the ways, because Alley, here, brought home some of the skunk's stink!"

"How are we ever going to get him home, Uncle Walt?" Justi sighed.

"Well, we have some tomato juice in the camper we can pour over him. That is supposed to help get rid of the smell."

Uncle Walt went on to explain, "After we bathe him in the tomato juice and rinse him with some soap and water, and get him dry, we can put him in his kennel and put the kennel under the boat tarp in the bottom of the boat and he will be nice and cozy for the ride home. I'm afraid if we put him in the camper, we will never rid ourselves of the smell!"

Poor little Alley braved the double bath like a trooper. He seemed happy just to be back with the family again after his night of adventuring. He didn't even seem too disappointed to be kenneled for the ride home.

The skunk smell still lingered, but didn't seem to affect appetites when Aunt Mae called everyone for pancakes with huckleberry syrup, bacon and scrambled eggs.

Zoey made sure that Alley got a nice piece of bacon.

Christopher woke up bright and early the morning after the Fourth of July, anxious to surprise everyone with fish for breakfast.

He had caught some nice trout yesterday. He had cleaned them and packed them in ice so they would be nice and fresh this morning.

He could almost smell the fish frying in the pan, already.

As Christopher stepped out of the camper, into the crisp morning, he was aware that the campsite seemed to be somewhat rearranged.

The table with the cooler on it was tipped on its side. A plastic container of tableware and napkins was strewed out across the ground. Chairs were tipped over. Some clothes that were hanging on a line had been pulled to the ground. The cooler lay open. Ice was melting. His fish were gone!

A large brown bear was just polishing off the leavings of a loaf of bread by a pine tree about twelve feet away!

"GET!" shouted Christopher, as loud as he could.

He waved his hands in the air and hollered again loudly, "Get outa' here you THIEF!"

The bear looked up and woofed, "Chuff, Chuff!"

Christopher threw his hands up again. The bear took off, grunting and chuffing.

"I guess he got his belly full of my fish!" Christopher said to his father, who had joined him.

"Well, son, you're lucky he didn't decide to challenge you, I don't think you'd be a good match!"

"I guess you're right," said Christopher, "I just reacted. I guess I really didn't stop to think."

Grandpa came out of the fifth wheel, "I guess the bear decided to dine out this morning, so that means we'll be dining in….in town."

Chapter 10

The Long Ride Home

Justi sat in the back of the car all the way home, reading the book about Butch Cassidy. Zoey tried to interest her in some traveling games, like "I See with My Little Eye" and "Guess Who".

Justi was having none of it. The book was intriguing. Intermittently, Justi made small comments:

"Oh, my goodness!"

"This is sooo cool…."

"Wow……….."

Aunt Mae and Uncle Walter looked at each other in disbelief. "Was this truly Justi, with her face buried in a historical publication? Would this girl ever cease to amaze them?"

In contrast, Christopher was fitfully sleeping in the back seat on his way home.

His family had proceeded to clean up their campsite after the bear incident.

They stopped off at a local diner for breakfast on the way home, to find there was a long line of campers with the same idea.

They finally got a table after a long wait.

The restaurant, not expecting such a heavy crowd, was out of bacon and most sausage. They did have some extra spicy sausage.

They were also short on batter for waffles, but produced some passable French toast, and cold scrambled eggs.

Gramps and Christopher's dad complained that the coffee was lukewarm. The orange juice was the highlight of the meal.

Maybe it was the thought of trading his trout for the breakfast he ended up with, but half way home, Christopher developed severe stomach pains.

He couldn't get comfortable. His Grandmother produced some anti acid tablets, which seemed to help some. He fell into a fitful sleep.

Christopher dreamed he was on a train. It came to a screeching stop as train robbers crashed through the doors and held up the train.

Christopher jumped up from his seat and pulled off the robber's bandana, grabbing his gun. It was Butch Cassidy!

Everyone on the train looked at brave Christopher in awe! The train jerked again and started going, but the dynamite the robbers had set on the safe, blew up.

Christopher jumped awake. The vehicle was stopped at the side of the road. A tire had blown and his father and Grandpa were getting the spare tire out of the back of the SUV to change tires.

Darn, thought Christopher. I could have been a hero!

Chapter 11

Like Pieces to a Puzzle

Christopher was back to his normal self Friday morning. He was even happy to help his brother at Sixth Street Café. The truck came with groceries for the restaurant. Everything had to be checked off and stored.

Christopher didn't get out of the restaurant until 3:45 that afternoon. He was glad he told Justi he would meet her inside the library, so she wouldn't wait for him to begin research.

When he got to the library, Justi and Sean were busy working on a computer in the meeting room.

"Look here what I found, Christopher!" Justi almost squealed.

She showed him one of the books they had

checked out. "Butch Cassidy, My Brother" read the title.

She turned to page 145 where it showed a "WANTED" poster put out by the Pinkerton detectives that L. Parker had talked about in the letter.

She turned the page and showed a continuation of the "reward" information, stating that the Pinkerton's National Detective Agency Representing the American Bankers' Association was offering a $6,000 reward.

It went on to say that Butch Cassidy and companions had robbed the First National Bank of Winnemucca, Nevada, September 19, 1900. They made away with $31,000 in $20 gold coins, $1,200 in $5 and $10 gold coins, and the balance of a total $32,640 in paper currency, including one $50 bill.

Justi went on to explain, "Sean and I have been working out a timeline, looking at old trail maps on the internet, and checking mileage, and the speed a horse could be expected to travel, and, well, I'm just finishing up the calculations, so you will be able to see here for yourself. L. Parker, if he is the real Butch Cassidy, we think could have actually pulled this robbery and made it up here with at least part of the loot!"

Justi was busy adding numbers and putting the finishing touches on a piece of paper.

She kept looking at a map and mumbling to herself, and rechecking figures on the paper they had been working on.

Christopher looked over Justi's shoulder at the paper she and Sean had been working on.

"Here, said Justi, it's finished, see…"

She handed Christopher the paper.

On the paper was a timeline figured out for the assumed travel of L. Parker from Winnemucca, Idaho to Dudley, Idaho.

Christopher read the following from the paper in his hand:

Timeline for L. Parker travel from Winnemucca, NV. To Dudley, ID

Robbed bank September 19, 1900

Roughly 600 miles old roads in 1900 to railroad spur between Lolo Pass and Missoula Montana

Figure 20 to 30 miles per day horseback (but he could have taken a train part of the way)

A month for longest - Figuring 600 / 20

Letter dated October 23, 1900............Yes, the letter could be right.

Christopher's face lit up with a knowing smile.

He explained, "Everything is fitting together. This is just like putting together a puzzle. Remember when the letter said that they had stopped at Dudley, where they saw the Pinkertons and rode the ferry to a mission?"

Christopher continued, "Well, when we were fishing, we met an old timer. He said that the Dudley, Idaho that L. Parker wrote of in his letter, is now a ghost town, but that it used to have a train station. There was also a ferry that went across the river to the Mission of the Sacred Heart."

"I guess we need to get online and see exactly how to get to the Old Mission, and if it is still accessible to the public."

"No problem there," said Justi. "The other book I checked out had lots of information on the Cataldo Mission. It is actually the oldest building in Idaho and it is not that far from here. It is now a state park."

Sean interrupted, "Hey, do you guys mind if I come along?"

"I have wheels if you need a ride, nothing fancy, but it will get you there. I also have a metal detector, which I'm thinking, might be good."

Justi and Christopher both agreed that it would be good to have Sean along. He knew the area and had been such a help so far, it seemed only fair. Besides, he had a car.

It was agreed that they would try to get together the next day, which would be Saturday. They looked up the Cataldo Mission hours and agreed to meet at the library at 1:00 p.m.

Sean added that he would throw in some shovels. They all agreed that they should wear hiking boots and bring gloves.

Chapter 12

Problems and Discoveries

Christopher arrived early at the library the next day. It was Sean's day off, so Christopher decided to spend the extra time by doing some more research online.

Christopher scanned websites on the Cataldo Mission. As he read more about the Cataldo Mission becoming a state park, a thought came to him.

"If the Mission is a state park, we probably need permission to do any treasure hunting, even if it is just with a metal detector."

He checked further, and found that in state parks in the State of Idaho, you need permission from the park ranger to do any metal detecting.

Christopher called the Cataldo Mission and found that the park ranger was not on duty on

Saturdays. The assistant ranger deferred to the park ranger's decision. That meant they would have to wait until a weekday to talk to the park ranger before any treasure hunting could take place.

When Justi and Sean arrived, Christopher explained the situation.

"Well, that doesn't mean we can't at least go over there and survey the situation," Justi mused.

"Okay, then, let's load up," interjected Sean.

Sean was enjoying the intrigue. He couldn't wait to see if Christopher and Justi actually had something here with this old letter and all.

He thought to himself, "Chances are, this is just a wild goose chase. Someone could have written a fake letter for a joke. Then, again, it looks real enough."

When they arrived at the Mission, they realized that there was another problem with their plan.

The landscape at the Cataldo Mission had changed immensely since the letter was written.

There was no sign of a ferry to the Mission. There were no riverboats in the river. The river now was too shallow to support large riverboats.

Large cedar trees that once stood by the water's edge were now stumps, or non-existent. Birch, cottonwood and several species of pine stood in their place.

The Mission, itself, stood much the same. If you stood off the left front porch, facing mostly north and slightly to the west, you looked out at a new interpretive center.

Unfortunately, the interpretive center somewhat obscured the view of the water below. No old railroad tie fence post stood in the foreground.

They were going to have to do some good guessing.

When they walked toward the water, it was apparent there was no longer a large beaver house in the eddy, which had also changed somewhat from old pictures they had found on the internet.

They looked at each other, a little dejected.

"Well, let's not give up yet," surmised Christopher.

"They may have dug anything up that was buried when they built the educational center."

They may have completely missed seeing an old hatbox. It could be anywhere, now."

"However, the educational center is a little more to the front of the Mission, and more north than I think Parker was describing, and still quite ways above the water."

"Remember, Parker said he walked down to a grove of *"fir saplings"* the priests had planted. It seems reasonable to think that at least some of those trees may still be standing."

Sean suggested, "Maybe if we follow that trail, with signs on it over there, to the west, we can see more down over the hill. Maybe something that looks like what he described in his letter."

They all agreed to the plan, and headed down the hill on a trail that headed in a westward direction.

Just past a display of an old grain mill, Justi let out a little squeal, "Look! We found the old mission cemetery!"

"Didn't Parker say he walked past this?"

"Look, look down there! See those three really tall fir trees just below the cemetery?"

"Doesn't that look like they could be almost in the right spot?"

"Possibly, agreed Christopher." Sean nodded his head in agreement.

They all hurried down the hill on the trail, past the remaining headstones.

The trail continued down the hill, winding its way past two very large fir trees. A little to the left, stood one more, very large fir. All of the trees were over three feet wide at the base and easily stood over 100 feet tall.

The path wound only a short ways down to the river. There were signs designating the old river channel and various species of trees.

Justi paused where the path wound between two of the large trees. She spoke with eager anticipation, "This is totally incredible! Just to think that I might be standing where Butch Cassidy stood about one-hundred-twenty years ago!"

They traced their way back up the hill to the Mission, making plans to contact the park ranger when the Mission opened the next day to get permission to use the metal detector.

Chapter 13

The Old Mission

Decisions by governmental agencies are never made overnight.

The park ranger, after being contacted the following Monday, advised that he needed to talk with the park manager and the archeologist, employed by the Coeur d'Alene Indian Tribal Council.

The next Monday, the seventeenth of July, Christopher had a message to call the park ranger. The ranger advised Christopher that the group could meet to discuss the request, that Wednesday, July nineteenth, if everyone could attend.

He requested that Christopher and Justi bring the letter from L. Parker, and at least one parent or guardian for each. Sean, being of age, would not require a guardian.

The park ranger went on to say that they needed to put their request for exploration and possible excavation in writing, identifying the area they were interested in, and the reason for it.

Christopher was beside himself. He hung up the phone.

"Grams, I have to run over to Justi's house for a few minutes. I'll be back for dinner."

"Well, you'd better get a move on, then," answered Grandma. "Dinner will be on the table in one hour."

Christopher grabbed his bicycle and sped over to see Justi. His head was whirling.

"Oh man! We have a lot of explaining to do to Dave and Jennifer, Walt and Mae and Grams and Gramps, and our parents before Wednesday!"

"I wonder if Justi is good at writing letters."

When Christopher got to Justi's house, he found Justi in the back yard playing with Zoey and the kitten.

"Christopher! Come See!"

Zoey was teaching the kitten to follow her through her plastic play tunnel in her play yard. She was coaxing it using a toy mouse tied to a string.

The kitten pounced joyfully on the mouse, picking it up in his mouth, and ran further into the tunnel after Zoey. Zoey crawled out the other side, giggling.

Christopher explained his conversation with the park ranger from the Old Mission State Park to Justi.

"Well," said Justi, "I think it's time we let everyone in on our discovery, anyway."

"I'll get Auntie and Uncle to come over to your Grams and Gramps tonight after dinner."

"Can you call Dave and Jennifer and ask them if they can meet over there, also?"

"Okay, Justi, that sounds great," replied Christopher.

"I'll get a letter typed up on Aunt Mae's

computer," added Justi.

Things were getting complicated, but at least they were getting somewhere.

Chapter 14

Council at the Interpretive Center

On the day of the meeting, Justi went to the Old Mission early with her aunt, uncle and little cousin, Zoey.

They toured the interpretive center and the Old Mission, itself.

"This is amazing," Justi whispered.

"The work it must have taken is hard to imagine! The whole ceiling of this Old Mission was stained blue as the sky by smashing thousands of wild huckleberries and using the juice!"

"The mission was built with the hands of the local Native Americans and the Jesuits without using nails, only wooden pegs. The boards were all hand hewn with axes."

She also read that the Mission was more than just a Catholic Mission. It was a way station on the old Mullan Road for travelers, both Native American and white; fur traders, immigrants, miners, and the military.

The Mission was also instrumental in forging a communications bridge between the Indians and Military during a time of upheaval for the local tribes.

Justi read that in 1858, the Cataldo Mission was the site of a council for peace negotiations between the Coeur d'Alene Tribe and Colonel George Wright, ending their participation in the Northern Plateau War.

"Wow! Now we are having another council to determine if we can bring some of our past to the surface, and how to do it with respect. How all of this is conducted, again, depends upon a *council* held at the same location as that *council* so many years ago!" thought Justi.

Just as Justi was about to check out another room in the interpretive center, she ran into Christopher, who was enjoying visual displays of the local tribes and the history of their life in the area.

"Justi, did you know that my great grandfather was raised on the Coeur d'Alene reservation?" asked Christopher.

"He went to the Native American Mission School in DeSmet, Idaho. The school was built there when they closed the school at the Cataldo Mission in 1892. I didn't know the year it was built, or that DeSmet was tied to the Cataldo Mission until I started reading about the Cataldo Mission history for our research."

"I remember my dad said his father never liked to talk much about school, except to say that he had to live away from home at the school and he got really lonely, and they were strict and he had to learn lots of new rules. It must have been hard for him."

Christopher continued, "When I was a little kid, I remember Great Gramps used to tell me bedtime stories about the trickster, Mr. Coyote, also stories about a silly Raven that acted like a clown, and was not too honest sometimes. They were always fun stories, but I think there was always a lesson I learned from those stories, most of all, how to be honest and care for nature. I miss my great grandfather and my great grandmother."

Christopher was lost in thought as he went on, "My great grandmother married my great grandfather when she was just seventeen years old. She helped cook at a logging camp where my great grandfather worked as a logger near Saint Maries, Idaho."

"I can remember her showing me beautiful doeskin boots decorated with many miniature blue beads, all hand sewn in the pattern of flowers. Her mother made them for her when she was sixteen. She used porcupine quills for needles to stitch through the deerskin."

"Great Granny said the beaded flowers were supposed to represent blue camas flowers, like the camas that grows in the forest meadows around here. She said the Indians used to eat the bulbs of the flower, digging the bulbs with elk antlers and roasting the flower bulb in pits dug into the earth. The bulbs are actually very high in protein. Grandpa says they are higher in protein than a steelhead trout."

Justi was surprised. "I didn't know you had any

tribal heritage! That is so cool! Does your father or your grandfather tell stories?"

Christopher was thinking, "Yes, Grandpa does when we go camping and I think Dad has talked about writing a book with some of the stories in it. I hope he does write them down so I can have them for my children."

Sean walked in the door just then, with a big smile on his face. "Okay, let's get the show on the road. I hope they serve refreshments!"

Christopher, Justi, Sean, Justi's aunt and uncle, with little Zoey all took seats in the large meeting room at the interpretive center.

A few minutes later, at exactly four p.m., Christopher's grandparents, along with his brother and sister-in-law, came in the door with Madelyn, the archeologist representing the Coeur d'Alene Tribal Council and Anna, the manager of the Old Mission State Park.

After some discussion, and after examining the letter from L. Parker, and viewing the ancient skeleton key, both women agreed that they would first need to explore the site where the letter and key were found to determine authenticity.

Dave and Jennifer agreed that they could meet at Sixth Street Café that Friday evening.

Justi and Christopher were excited to show everyone the hidden room in the basement. Maybe there were more artifacts they had missed!

Sean interjected, "Does that mean that I'm invited too? I love exploring spooky old places!"

Dave added, "Yes, Sean, you too. We have brooms for all three of you detectives."

Madelyn, the archeologist, added, "No cleaning down there until we check out the wall and the room. The less disturbed it is, the better chance we have of establishing how old the wall, the trunk, and items in the trunk are. Hopefully, there are other relics in the room that will help us establish a time period."

She added, "We have checked the letter, and are fairly certain it is authentic."

"I am also familiar with the building the café is in. It was constructed in 1890 and it is certainly old enough to have been standing and in operation at the time the letter was written. So, we shall see."

Chapter 15

Just Like Pirates – or Maybe Not

Friday evening, at four p.m., the archeologist, Madelyn, met with Dave, Jennifer, Christopher, Justi and Sean in the basement of Sixth Street Café.

Madelyn was able to confirm that the trunk and clothing most likely came from the same time period as the letter.

She noted that the envelope, though bent and torn, also looked correct for that period of time. She also pointed out that the postmark was hand stamped and looked like it was stamped in Spokane, Washington.

"See here, it looks like October 25, 1900."

They searched for other relics, but found no more clues in the old room. The shelves contained only old jars and crockery. All were from an earlier time period, but probably not as early as 1900. Madelyn believed the jars and crockery were probably the 1920s or 1930s vintage.

"It's hard to say when the trunk was brought in here, or why the wall was sealed off," Madelyn stated thoughtfully.

As she talked, she began pushing on different areas of the wood wall behind the shelf. Dust crumbled from the wall and the shelf creaked. The whole wall moved. The shelf hid a door on the other side of the wall. The door opened stubbornly creaking with age. The door led into the cave-like portion of the basement.

"It looks like this was a secret door, hiding this room. It was probably walled up during the late 1920s or 1930s, which would have been during the prohibition period when it was illegal in the United States to purchase or sell alcoholic beverages. Some people manufactured the alcohol illegally during that period and stored it in hidden in places like this." Madelyn continued, as much talking to herself, as to the group in the room:

"We can just assume that the trunk was stored here before the room was closed off, which would mean it was put in here sometime between 1900 and 1920."

"Everything about the letter and where it was found seems valid. I see no reason why Anna and I shouldn't move ahead with planning an excavation of a small area around the site, and present the plans to the Council, who will have the final say."

That night, Justi, her aunt and uncle, little Zoey, and Justi's parents, who had returned from Maine, all met at Christopher's grandparent's house for dinner and a little pre-emptive celebration. Christopher's parents had come up for the weekend. Dave and Jennifer were also there.

Jennifer, being very pregnant, looked like she had a basketball under her shirt. She was extremely uncomfortable with the summer heat, and spent a lot of time with her shoes off and her feet up.

At dinner, Christopher related to the rest of the

family what Madelyn, the archeologist had outlined as the plan to proceed forward.

"She says it may take weeks, even months for everything to be authorized, but seemed optimistic that we can start before we have to go back to school."

"You mean we get to dig for treasure, just like pirates?" piped up Zoey.

"Well, no, not quite like that." Christopher advised.

"Things have changed a lot from the old days. They want to be careful not to disturb places that are important to the culture of any of the people that previously inhabited the area, just like you wouldn't want someone to come into your room and start digging around without your permission, would you?"

"Well, no," said Zoey, "But that man put that stuff there. He dug too!"

"Yes, but he didn't know what he was doing," responded Justi.

"Now, we know we have to be careful and follow

the rules to get it removed, if anything is really there."

"We just have to be very patient."

Chapter 16

Somewhere It Waits

Little did Justi know how true her words were, when she told Zoey that she had to be very patient.

The long, hot month of August came and went.

Each time Justi and Christopher went to the library, Sean greeted them with an anxious, expectant look.

"Have you heard any word from the Mission?"

Their answer was always the same.

"No word."

Justi and Christopher had to leave, the end of August, to go back to North River for school.

They still had no answer on when the dig might take place.

Madelyn, the archeologist, had stopped answering their plaintive entreaties to "hurry things up!"

The leaves were coming down in droves. Justi and her sister, Kate, were raking the yard, making huge piles of leaves, only to have them scattered by their rambunctious golden retriever, Tater.

Christopher drove up in his dad's car. He had a big grin on his face.

"Guess who just called?"

"No way! Was it Madelyn?" Justi dropped her rake and her jaw simultaneously.

"YUP!" responded Christopher.

"She said the date is set for Saturday, October fourteenth. They planned it for a Saturday so we can attend with our families. They are closing the park for that day. I just got off the phone with Sean. He was pretty smug because he had just found out from the park manager, himself. He tried not to show it, but, you know Sean. I'll bet he is so excited he is out there at five in the morning on the fourteenth!"

It was hard for Justi and Christopher to think of anything else for the next couple of weeks. Their families had been sworn to secrecy, so they couldn't talk about the coming event to anyone but each other.

The time passed quickly, however, with school in session.

While walking home from school, on Friday, October, thirteenth, Christopher asked Justi, "So, are you ready for the unveiling?"

"Well, yes," sighed Justi, "I have been ready for this dig for months. Just think, somewhere, out there, under a few layers of dirt, maybe a treasure lies in wait. It waits to be discovered and brought to light."

"Well," shared Christopher, "I'm just glad it's not today, Friday the thirteenth, that we are digging that treasure up, or on Halloween! There's just no telling what we might dig up with the treasure!"

Just then a bat flew by, screeching.

"Wow, that was truly weird," exclaimed Christopher."

"Not so much," assured Justi.

"There is that old cave in the mountain just a couple of blocks up that used to have an old elevator shaft to the house on the hill. There are bats hanging around the cave all the time, even though there is a door on it and it is locked. I think there are holes the bats get in and out of."

October the fourteenth was there before they knew it. Everyone arrived at the site at nine o'clock a.m.

Justi, Christopher and Sean were surprised to find the specific site already had been determined with a metal detector, and had been lined out with flags and ropes. There were markings where they planned to dig. Two young interns from the university were standing by with gloves and shovels. Madelyn seemed to be giving them last minute instructions.

Chairs had been provided for onlookers under a portable canopy. Coffee and juice were provided. There was a photographer from the

Tribal Cultural Center.

Justi recognized one of Idaho's Senators and a Representative talking to the Chairman of the Coeur d'Alene Tribe. She also saw the park manager, Anna, helping with arrangements.

The local sheriff was there, talking to the park ranger. There were also some other policemen Justi didn't recognize.

The excavation had started. Everyone fell silent. They dug very carefully and extremely slow, stopping every few minutes to inspect. All of a sudden, they called Madelyn over to check something.

After looking over the diggings for a few moments, she told them to get hand tools and dig slowly around.

Moments later, it was apparent they had unearthed something soft and loose. They continued their painstakingly slow brushing off and hand digging with small tools.

Madelyn finally gave them the signal to stop digging.

The photographer moved forward as Madelyn reached into the hole and gently lifted a stiff and bundled piece of canvas-like material, crumpled in a ball, covered with age, sandy damp earth and roots.

As dirt fell away, she set it down and slowly unfolded the ball. Inside, was a moldy, blackish-brown lump of leather. It was what used to be an old oval hatbox. Interestingly, important parts of the hatbox still seemed to be intact, when the dirt and roots were brushed off carefully.

The lid of the old hatbox still actually resembled a lid. There was a latch with a lock. The lock was still in place.

"Christopher, did you remember the key?" queried Madelyn.

"Here it is!" responded Christopher, pulling the miniature skeleton key, complete with a red cord that had been tied around it when it was found.

Madelyn turned the key in the rusty lock. It stuck a couple of times. Someone poured a little oil on the lock. They tried it again.

To everyone's surprise, it opened!

Inside, there were many discolored gold coins. One of the interns picked up one of the coins.

"It is a twenty-dollar gold piece! We have found the actual treasure!"

The hatbox was carefully removed from its ancient bed. They set it on a table near the site, for all to view. Madelyn carefully removed the twenty-dollar gold pieces from inside the crumbling hatbox.

She stacked them carefully in piles of five. Everyone silently counted as each was removed and inspected. In all, there were one hundred gold coins.

Packed neatly between the gold coins, Madelyn removed one fifty-dollar gold certificate and three twenty-dollar gold certificates. The date on them read 1882.

The treasure, spread out on the table was an intriguing sight as slices of the gold coins, shining through years of corrosion, sparkled in the late morning sun.

A gold certificate waved in the light breeze that had come up. It flipped over and danced off the table, as if Butch Cassidy was snatching it up, one last time.

"To think all of this lay just a few feet below so many feet that walked that path for over 100 years!" Madelyn exclaimed.

"Thank you, Justi, Christopher and Sean, for your undying curiosity and perseverance in helping to uncover this historic find.

Chapter 17

The Bounty and the Great Divide

July Fourth, the following year, found several
changes in the lives of Justi, Christopher and
Sean.

Sean Kellogg now held a part time position as
computer technologist at the Cataldo Mission's
Educational/Interpretive center, as well as his
regular job at Silver Creek Public Library.

Christopher was now an uncle.

Little Mark had been born in the middle of
September after Justi and Christopher went back
to North River. He was just now starting to walk.
Justi's niece, Zoey, being a year older, considered
herself to be "a big girl" now.

They frequently found Zoey with her little hands
on her hips, telling little Mark what to do:

"No Markie! Don't pull the kitty's tail!"

"Markie, here, hold kitty, but don't slobber all over him!"

"No, Markie, you can't eat my mud pies!"

Sixth Street Café was now an internet café. Business had picked up and Justi and Christopher were trying to talk Dave and Jennifer into adding a small library of books for patrons to read or borrow.

Christopher and Justi were local celebrities in Silver Creek. They, along with Sean, were overjoyed to learn that they had been gifted with a trip to Washington D.C. with their parents and family to visit the White House to meet the President, the State of Idaho's governor, Idaho's two senators and two representatives, along with the Chairman of the Coeur d'Alene Tribal Council in appreciation of their historical discovery.

A classroom, complete with twelve computers, books and displays for use by local schools on Salish heritage, wildlife, and native plant species had been added to the Mission Interpretive

Center.

An addition was created, called "Alley's Alley" at the local shelter for homeless cats, complete with outside play yard in recognition of Alley's part in the discovery.

Two of the twenty dollar gold pieces were put on display at the Cataldo Mission educational center, with a picture of Justi, Christopher, Sean, the archeologist, the park ranger, the state park manager, and the Chairman of the Schit su'umsh or Coeur d'Alene Tribal Council as the discovery was unveiled.

Dave and Jennifer donated the old trunk and clothing from the basement of the Sixth Street Café, where the letter was found, to the Silver Creek Museum.

The details of the disposition of the coins and paper money from the bank robbers were still being worked out between governmental officials.

Justi and Christopher were surprised to find that the worth of the fifty-dollar gold certificate raised the most in value, as a collector's item.

The town of Silver Creek erected a bronze statue of L. Parker, standing, with his horse at his side. Two teenagers, a boy and a girl, with a kitten beside them, stood looking out in awe in the direction he pointed.

They were looking out over the Valley, planning their next quest.......somewhere.

The Mission of the Sacred Heart

Old Mission State Park

Cataldo, Idaho

Wild Camas Flowers in the Spring

ABOUT THE AUTHOR

Eloise and her husband, Doug are both natives of Northern Idaho.

They raised their four children in the Boise area and returned to the Cataldo area in North Idaho to retire.

When not writing, Eloise keeps busy working part time at the local library, gardening, judging small animals for 4-H and FFA, and enjoying the outdoors with her husband.

When the grandchildren come to visit, she always has a new story to tell them, or an idea for an adventure in the mountains.

Eloise and Doug share their home with three spoiled dogs, eight chickens and one very spoiled cat.

AUTHOR'S NOTE

Justi Wallace and Christopher Williams had previous adventures in this author's first fiction novel called:

JUSTI'S GOING NOWHERE (*Justi Wallace, Teen Almost*)
This book was written for a younger audience. Justi and Christopher were also younger..
This book could be a worthwhile and quick read to fill you in on the background of this pair of young detectives.

Secret to Somewhere

www.ingramcontent.com/pod-product-compliance
Lightning Source LLC
Chambersburg PA
CBHW030539130626
46552CB00006B/2338